Johnny Appleseed

retold by Carol Ottolenghi   illustrated by CD Hullinger

Copyright © 2004 McGraw-Hill Children's Publishing. Published by Brighter Child, an imprint of McGraw-Hill Children's Publishing, a Division of The McGraw-Hill Companies. Send all inquiries to: McGraw-Hill Children's Publishing, 8787 Orion Place, Columbus, Ohio 43240-4027. Made in the USA.   ISBN 0-7696-3281-5   1 2 3 4 5 6 7 8 9 PHXBK 09 08 07 06 05 04

The McGraw-Hill Companies

People tell plenty of tall tales about Johnny Appleseed. But he was a real person, same as you and me. His name was John Chapman.

John was born on September 26, 1774, in a small town in Massachusetts.

John had ten brothers and sisters. Whenever he wanted some quiet time for thinking, he'd head for the woods.

John learned to read and write, which not everybody did in those days. He also learned to tend apple orchards.

John loved the smell of the orchard and the crisp sweetness of the apples. And helping the trees grow from seedlings to mature trees showed him how human beings and nature could work together. In fact, it gave him an idea.

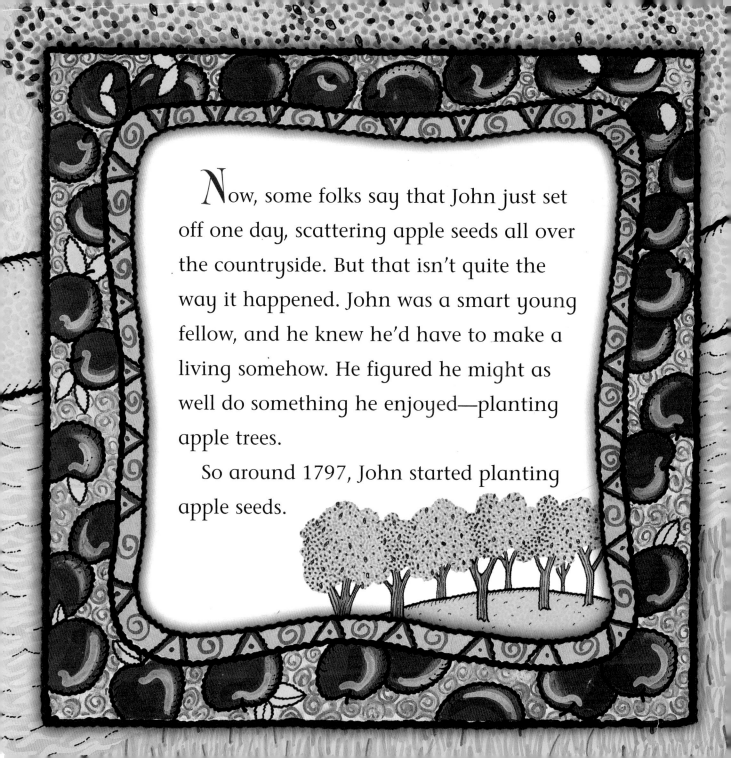

Now, some folks say that John just set off one day, scattering apple seeds all over the countryside. But that isn't quite the way it happened. John was a smart young fellow, and he knew he'd have to make a living somehow. He figured he might as well do something he enjoyed—planting apple trees.

So around 1797, John started planting apple seeds.

John was one of the first white people to explore the Northwest Territory. He discovered that the area had rich soil, great for growing apples.

By the time settlers arrived, the apple trees in
John's nurseries were big enough to sell. Folks soon
started calling him "The Apple Tree Man." And it
wasn't long before he was known everywhere as
Johnny Appleseed.

Apple trees were important to life on the new frontier. In fact, a law was made that said every family had to plant 50 apple trees on their homestead.

You see, back then settlers grew almost everything they ate. Apples became a mighty big part of their diets. They used the apples to make cider, pies, and applesauce. They even fed apples to their animals!

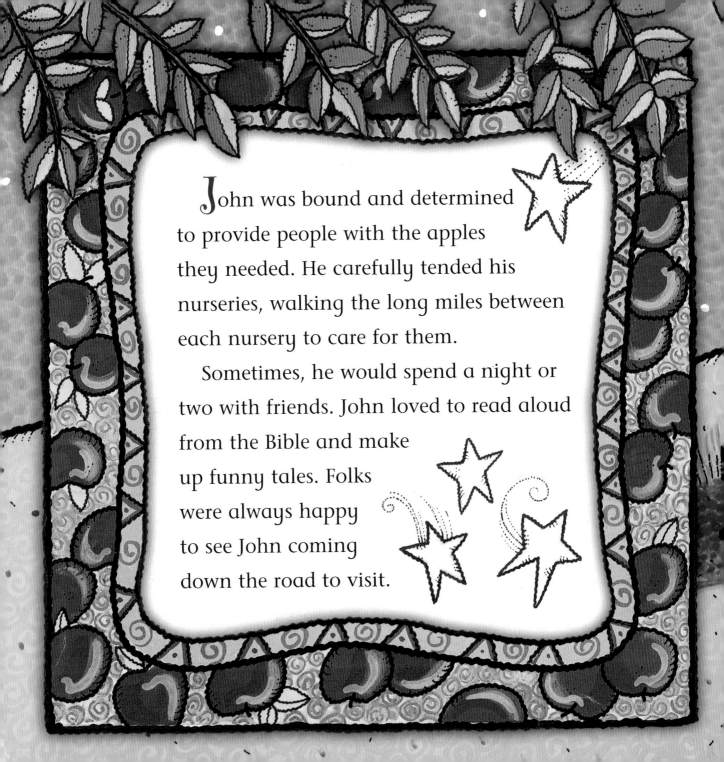

John was bound and determined to provide people with the apples they needed. He carefully tended his nurseries, walking the long miles between each nursery to care for them.

Sometimes, he would spend a night or two with friends. John loved to read aloud from the Bible and make up funny tales. Folks were always happy to see John coming down the road to visit.

Every fall, John got apple seeds from the cider mills. The mills pressed apples for juice, then threw out the seeds and peels.

John would plant these seeds in the spring. Then, he would build a fence around the nursery to keep hungry critters from eating his tender young trees.

John treated everyone with respect, and folks respected him. He made friends with the Native Americans.

He got to be such good friends with the local tribes that when lightning started fires in John's nurseries, they battled the flames right alongside him.

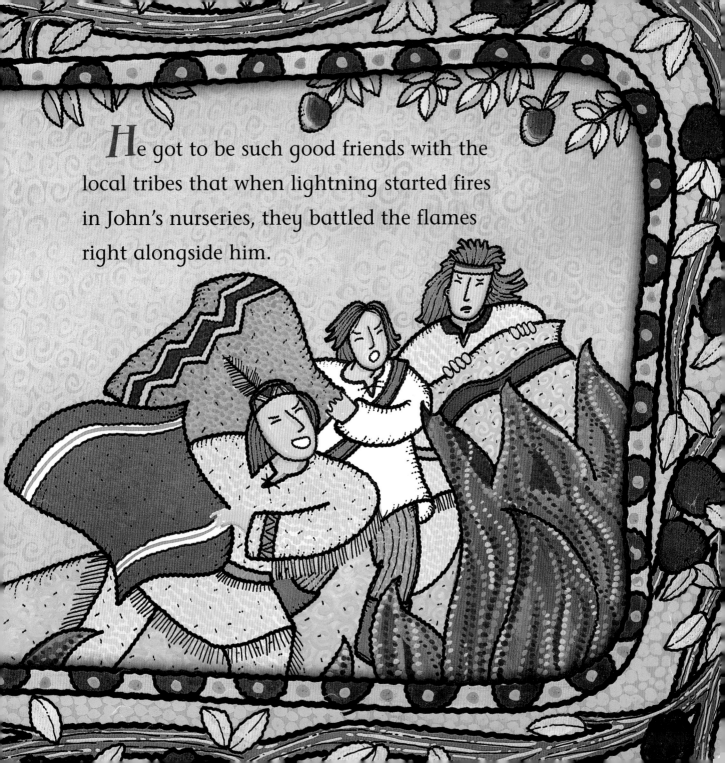

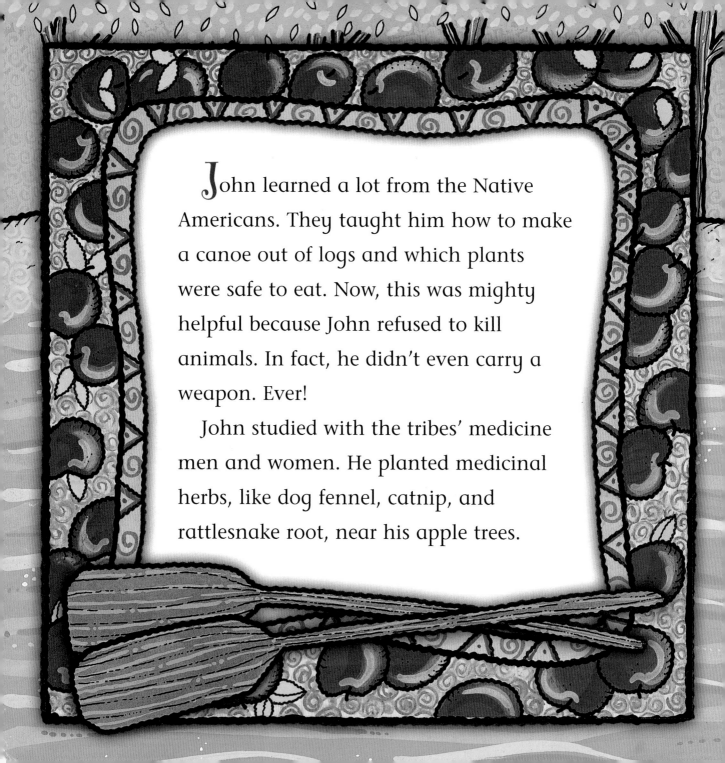

John learned a lot from the Native Americans. They taught him how to make a canoe out of logs and which plants were safe to eat. Now, this was mighty helpful because John refused to kill animals. In fact, he didn't even carry a weapon. Ever!

John studied with the tribes' medicine men and women. He planted medicinal herbs, like dog fennel, catnip, and rattlesnake root, near his apple trees.

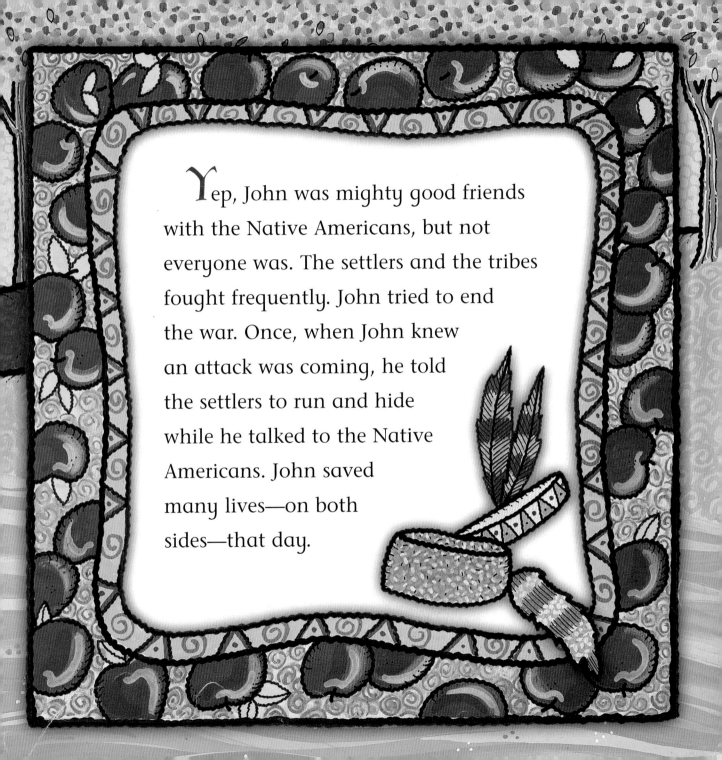

Yep, John was mighty good friends with the Native Americans, but not everyone was. The settlers and the tribes fought frequently. John tried to end the war. Once, when John knew an attack was coming, he told the settlers to run and hide while he talked to the Native Americans. John saved many lives—on both sides—that day.

John traveled the frontier planting apple trees for almost fifty years. He never married, but many friends loved and admired him. He was staying with friends in Indiana when he heard that cows were trampling one of his nurseries. It was a cold night, but John set out right away.

It turned out the night was too cold. John caught a disease folks called *the winter plague*. He died on March 18, 1845.

After John died, folks started telling tall tales about him. They said he wrestled with bears...

...And a wolf adopted him as a pet.

They said that John slept up in his apple trees and that the birds sang him to sleep.

They said that John never wore shoes, even in winter.

All that barefoot walking made his feet tough. Some folks said John's feet got so tough that they'd break the fangs off any snake silly enough to bite him.

Why, folks even said they saw John wearing a pot for a hat! There were all kinds of stories about Johnny Appleseed. Some were true. Some were not.

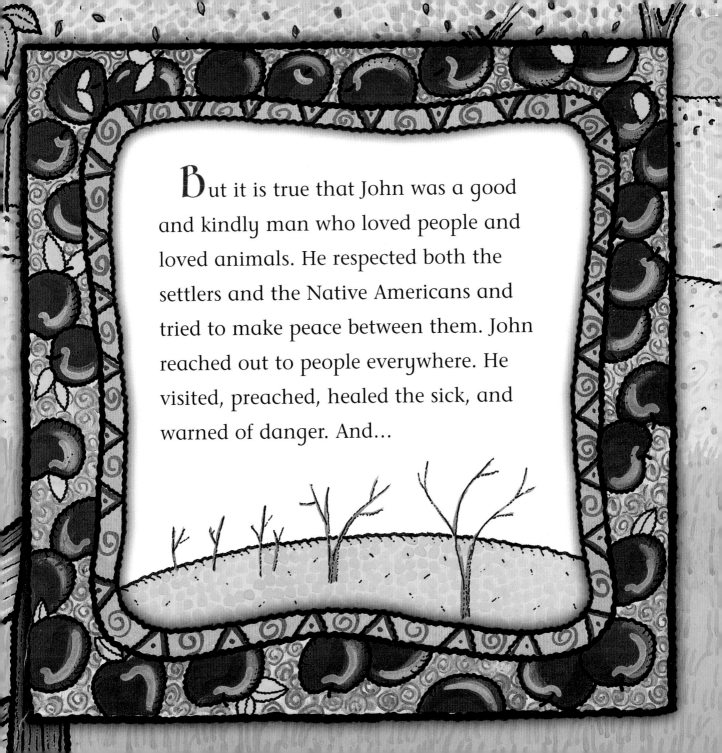

But it is true that John was a good and kindly man who loved people and loved animals. He respected both the settlers and the Native Americans and tried to make peace between them. John reached out to people everywhere. He visited, preached, healed the sick, and warned of danger. And...

...Always, always, he planted his apple seeds.